Mama Zooms

Written and illustrated by
Jane Cowen-Fletcher

SCHOLASTIC INC.
New York Toronto London Auckland Sydney

With heartfelt thanks to Brad
for your love and support and for making this possible,
and to
Bruce McMillan
for making it a reality

ISBN 0-590-45775-6

12 11 10 9 8 7 6 5 4 4 5 6 7 8/9

Printed in the U.S.A. 08

Design by Kristina Iulo

Pastel and colored pencil on
tinted pastel paper (Canson Mi-Tientes).

To Paula, Tim and Brice David
and the memory of
Bradley John

Mama's got a
zooming machine
and she zooms me
everywhere.

Every morning
Daddy puts me
in Mama's lap
and we're off!

Mama zooms me
across the lawn
and she's my
racehorse.

Mama zooms me
through a puddle
and she's my
ship at sea.

Mama zooms me
down a smooth sidewalk
and she's my
race car.

Mama zooms me
fast down ramps.
We love ramps!

Mama zooms me
across a bridge
and she's my
airplane.

Mama zooms me
through a dark hall
and she's my
train in a tunnel.

Mama zooms me
over a bumpy road
and she's my
buckboard wagon.

Mama zooms me
along the ocean boardwalk
and she's my wave.

Mama has
very strong arms
from all our zooming.

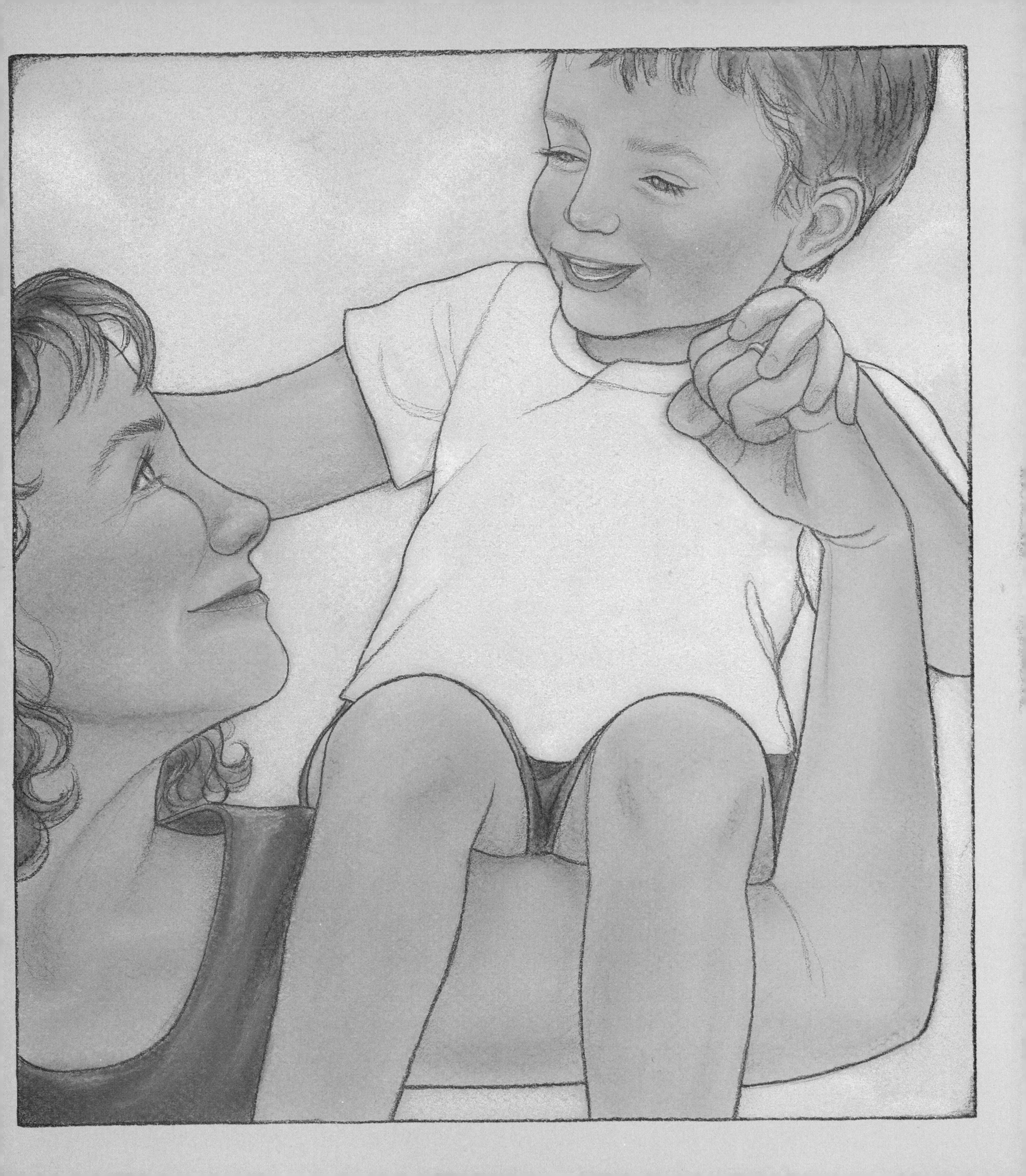

Daddy and I push her up
only the very steepest hills.
When we get to the top,
Daddy says, "See you
back on earth!"...

. . . And Mama zooms me
to the stars and she's
my spaceship.

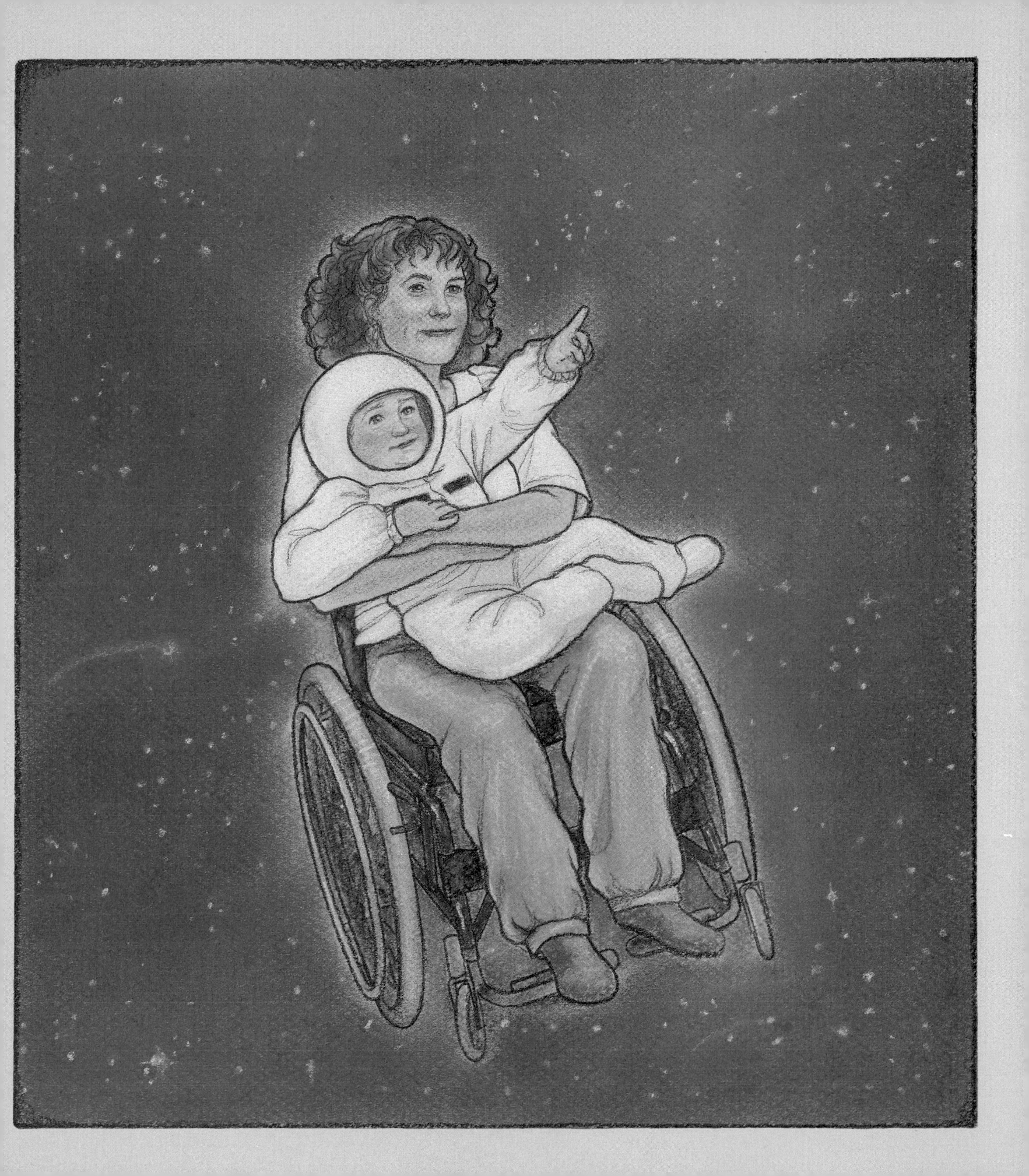

Mama zooms me
right up until bedtime.
Then Mama is just
my mama, and that's
how I like her best.